Curious Charlie Goes To The ZOO

ENTRY →

TIM ROBBINS

Second Edition 2022

ISBN: 978-1-915164-95-7 (Paperback)
　　　　978-1-915164-93-3 (Hardback)

Copyright © Tim Robbins

Written by: Tim Robbins

Cover by: White Magic Studios

Illustrated by: White Magic Studios

Designed by: White Magic Studios

Published by: Maple Publishers
　　　　　　　 1 Brunel Way, Slough, SL1 1FQ

Charlie wants to see if he can find his favourite animal, but along the way Charlie meets lots of different animals.

Can you help Charlie name them by solving the clues and matching them to the animals on the first page?

Also, throughout the book are hidden ladybirds, can you help find them all?

Charlie looks through the plants.

Charlie looks over the plants.

Far in the distance Charlie spots a horse!

No wait, he looks carefully, it has black and white stripes and it is eating plants.

What can it be thought Charlie?

Can you name this animal?

Charlie peeps over the rocks.

Charlie peeps under the rocks.

Suddenly a rock moves!!

Is it really a rock? It has four legs, a head that pokes out from it and it is eating lettuce.

What can it be thought Charlie?

Can you name this animal?

Charlie peers up at the trees.

Charlie checks around the trees.

Suddenly the leaves on the trees start to rustle. Charlie peers up again.

What is that? It has long arms; it is swinging from branch to branch and from tree to tree, whilst eating a banana.

What can it be thought Charlie?

Can you name this animal?

Charlie stares into the water.

Charlie has fun splashing in the water.

But something is floating in the water. Is it a log?

NO, Listen! SNAP, SNAP, SNAP, it has caught a fish with its sharp teeth.

What can it be thought Charlie?

Can you name this animal?

Charlie stomps in some mud, squelch, squelch!

Charlie bends down to pick up some mud.

Something catches Charlie's eye. Something is bathing in the mud.

14

It has an exceptionally large body, short stumpy legs, a tiny tail, and it can open its mouth very wide.

What can it be thought Charlie?

Can you name this animal?

Charlie whistles
loudly as he walks.

Charlie hears something
and looks up high into
the branches.

"Twit Twoo" it said. It has a mouse in its long talons; it has big round eyes, a brown flat face, wings, and it can almost turn its head all the way round.

What can it be thought Charlie?

Can you name this animal?

Charlie copies the next animal; he raises his outstretched arm to his nose and waves it about.

Next Charlie flaps his hands, backwards and forwards by his ears.

The animal looks surprised by Charlie.

This animal is grey with big ears, big feet and it squirts water at Charlie from its awfully long nose. Then it goes back to eating a mountain of food.

What can it be thought Charlie?

Can you name this animal?

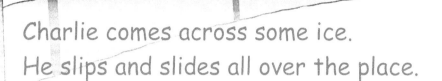

Charlie comes across some ice.
He slips and slides all over the place.

Wheeee! What fun Charlie was having especially when he lands on his bottom and skids across the ice.

Charlie is excited to see something has joined him on the ice.

This animal is particularly good at standing up on the ice. It is black and white, it has webbed feet and it likes eating fish.

What can it be thought Charlie?

Can you name this animal?

Curious Charlie continues his adventure, gazing up at the tall trees as he walks.

He grabs a fallen branch and throws it in the air, watching it go higher and higher. Charlie is shocked to see an animal.

It has the longest neck you have ever seen, and it is eating leaves from tops of trees.

What can it be thought Charlie?

Can you name this animal?

Charlie strolls on and suddenly
he opens his mouth and ROARS!

Charlie cups his hands around
his mouth and ROARS again only
this time it is much louder.

ROAR!!!

You will not believe what happens next! Charlie hears a ROAR, Charlie creeps up as quietly as he can and then he sees it. His favourite animal; the king of the jungle, with its long mane, sharp teeth, and claws.

Charlie knows this animal.

Can you name this animal?

Thank-you for helping curious Charlie during his adventure at the zoo. Curious Charlie wonders if you managed to name all the animals?

Which were your favourite animals?

Did you find all 23 hidden ladybirds?

CPSIA information can be obtained
at www.ICGtesting.com
Printed in the USA
BVHW020853230522
637794BV00007B/182

9 781915 164933